The child and Silence

John King

Tatterdemalion Blue

First published by **Tatterdemalion** Blue in 2014

Words © John King 2014
Illustrations © John King 2014

A CIP catalogue record for this book is available from the British Library

Cover design and layout by **Tatterdemalion** Blue

ISBN 978-0-9573315-1-8

Tatterdemalion Blue
8 Upper Bridge Street
Stirling
FK8 1ER

www.tatterdemalionblue.com

The child and Silence

For my Mum
Eileen

The child and Silence

Tinkle ...

Tinkle ...

Tinkle ...

Somewhere a tiny bell was ringing.

"Wake up Johnnie."

A Mother's voice was softly calling.

A child was asleep.

Johnnie was dreaming.

He did not know that he was dreaming
and much more than this

what he could not know

was that this was going to be
his greatest dream.

Tinkle ...

Tinkle ...

Tinkle ...

Johnnie opened his eyes within his dream
and all around him as far as he could see
was light.

A vast majesty of light

and he imagined
this must be the most beautiful of all
for within this light
all the many colours of the imagination
existed
and as each
of the many colours would fall
from the colour-seed would blossom
a flower
with fragrant petals blooming.
Sunlight
upon butterfly wings.
Swirling
a leaf of gold
spiralling the branches of a mighty tree
and beyond?

A bird in silent flight and silent song.

Moonlight
upon a dream meadow-glade
a mirror lake encircling.

Above?

A wild swan.
A white dove.

A forest and wild
of tiger stripes
and the lion's mane.
A wise elephant.
A monkey's smile.
Eyes shining.
Tears.
A drop of rain.
A rain-cloud and rain showers.
Waterfalls falling
thunder-mist valleys.
Illumined-spray and light-beams.
A rainbow bridge.
Cascading colour-streams.
A silent river
seeking.

The sea.

A turtle.
A dolphin.
Fishes that swim blue oceans.
Blue seas.
Blue sky reflection.
An eagle upon the breeze.
Wild white horses.
Bright white sands.
Dune-deserts
an oasis
wishing-well and palms.

A snowy mountain.
Snow clouds and snowflakes dancing.

Starlight.

Magical realms
palaces and castles.
All peoples and all kingdoms
great and small
alive in light and in life
and after all of these and more
a silent garden
amidst whose falling leaves
children were playing
dancing and singing.

All was Silence.

All was light

and of this silent light
all things were born
and to which
all things must return

for to each was given the Gift to life.

A moment of beauty.

A moment of perfection
prior to dissolving within the source
from whence they came.

Johnnie felt such peace

his being at one with the source
of this silent light
and he wished that he may stay

for he imagined
this must be his true home.

The Child King

Tinkle ...

Tinkle ...

Tinkle ...

In a twinkling as he blinked his eyes
all was transformed into darkness
and all of a sudden
although he knew not why
a fear grew in his heart.

He was alone.

The darkness was so overwhelming
he felt consumed by its depths
so overpowering
he began to struggle for breath

so much so
he felt he could no longer breathe.

The fear in his heart grew
and grew

until ...

Tinkle ...

Tinkle ...

Tinkle ...

Way, way far off in the distance
appeared the tiniest spark of a flame
speeding towards him
and in the twinkling of an eye
he gazed before him in wonder
of the most amazing sight
he had ever seen.

An Elephant Child King
whose smile alone
seemed to light the darkness
and in whose eyes
he imagined he saw many things.

Shooting stars and comets.
Suns and moons and planets.
Galaxies and universes
spiralling like white childlike angels
sent to adorn the darkness.

Johnnie reflected upon the darkness
and as he did so
the fear in his heart returned.

Upon seeing this
the Child King looked into his eyes
smiled and said

*"Johnnie you need not feel any fear
Mother is with you at all times.*

You are never alone."

Although he was unsure of the words
the words were soothing.

The fear was fading.

The Child King assured him

"She is your Mother too!"

"Johnnie."

He discerned of the sound
of the Mother's voice calling.

The Dance of Song

Tinkle ...

        Tinkle ...

                Tinkle ...

The sounds of the tinkling bell
seemed so beautiful
like a sacred music borne of the Silence
and as he gazed upon the darkness
the vision in the Child King's eyes
appeared before him.

Suns and moons and planets.
Shooting stars and comets.
Galaxies of spiralling universes
and with each new creation
a new sound
rebounding off the multitudinous bodies
lighting the night sky.

The universe was burning so brightly
alive with a melody flowing
like a mighty river to the sea.
A wave embracing Johnnie and raising him
ever higher and higher
and as he gazed all around him
he no longer knew any fear.
He felt so free.
Illumined in the light of this heavenly vision.

A seemingly never-ending story unfolding
filling him
with the vision of a spiralling creation
and the grace
of every nuance of every sound.

Johnnie and the Child King smiled
bowed
and with such ease
began the Dance of Song
as if they had always known of this moment.
And how they danced
borne
upon the waves of a celestial melody.

Gliding upon comets.
Tiptoeing across planets.
Sailing upon shooting stars.
Tripping so lightly the night sky
while skipping silently
beyond the gaze of the Sun and Moon.
Lost
within this most wondrous of all moments
raising them ever higher and higher
in circles spiralling the universe

when ...

Tinkle ...

Tinkle ...

Tinkle ...

Johnnie found himself alone.

Alone
amidst the fragrant petals of a flower
of the most exceeding beauty.
Soul white as the source
of the silent light
that lights the heavens
and all around him a great ocean.

He felt at peace.
The ocean appeared so still.
A mirror
offering her most perfect reflection
of the skies above
that shone in the splendour and glory
of the many twinkling stars and planets.

So still the ocean and skies
that the two seemed to be connected.
To be one.
He froze
for only a moment ago the Child King and he
had been happily dancing
within the midst of these heavenly bodies.

The Flower of Flowers

A gentle breeze blew across the ocean
touching him where he stood.

As it did so
it caused to ripple a wave across the petals
of this most exquisite of flowers.
A shimmering rainbow-wave of colours
each more beautiful than the next.

Johnnie wondered of the beauty
of this Flower of Flowers.
An almost overwhelming beauty
and yet
although the serene setting
and the mere presence of the flower
exuded peace
he was once more very aware
of his being alone.

A hint of fear arose in his heart.
The breeze blew.

He felt troubled.
The ocean was disturbed.
The winds began to blow.

24

The fear grew.
The skies filled with storm-clouds.

Thunder roared and lightning crackled
zigzagging the heavens.

Waves formed upon the seas
while the winds
forced the petals of the flower
to rise and fall
creating monster-like shadows
all around him.

The furthermost petals
like a many headed hooded serpent
looming ominously over him.

Johnnie was powerless.

The fear gripped his heart
as the rains from the seas and skies
lashed down upon him.

Tinkle ...

Tinkle ...

Tinkle ...

At the height of the storm
he heard the sound of the tiny bell
and although helpless it seemed to him
that as the fear in his heart grew
so it was the darkness reigned.

The fear became the creator
of the shadowy monsters
and perhaps
the many headed hooded serpent
was simply the petals rising
offering him their protection.

Yet he could not contain the fear
which in his heart grew.

The storm raged on.

In the midst of the furore
the Child King's voice calm and sure
commanded

"Be still!"

All was silent.

The great ocean serene
once more offering the most perfect reflection
of the starlit heavens above.
A rainbow-wave rippled the Flower of Flowers
whose furthermost petals were now simply
the most gentle support
cushioning her presence
upon the waters of the great ocean.

By his side stood the Child King
whose being alone assuaged his fear.
The Child King looked into his eyes
smiled and said

"Johnnie, do not be fearful
Mother is with you at all times.
She would never allow any harm to befall you."

The words seemed to soothe him.

Johnnie felt such peace
and in the Child King's eyes
he imagined he saw many things.

The birth of the earth
blue skies
clouds
snows and rains.
Flowing rivers
valleys
forests and mountains.
Animals
mammals
fishes great and small.
Songbirds.
Seabirds.
All birds of flight.
The most graceful of which
appeared to carry him
over realms and kingdoms
filled and flowing with all peoples

when ...

A noise disturbed his reverie.

A sound
like the far distant flapping of wings.

He gazed now into the distance
where appeared
the tiniest speck upon the horizon
which grew
and grew
until before his eyes
he perceived of the most beautiful bird
he had ever seen.

A Golden Eagle who in a moment
had alighted upon the Flower of Flowers

smiling graciously
upon Johnnie and the Child King.

The Golden Eagle

The Flower of Flowers
upon receiving his presence
sent a shimmering rainbow-wave of colours
flowing across her petals.

Johnnie was in awe
for as he gazed upon this bejewelled eagle
he became aware
of two of the most luxurious seats
placed between his wings
adorned with the finest silk raiment
of yellow and gold.

He gazed upon the Child King
and then upon himself and began to smile
for they too were attired
in pure yellow and gold silk finery.

They bowed together and began to laugh
dancing and singing
as they helped one another to climb aboard
this most illustrious of birds.
Who
upon seeing them safely seated
with such ease and grace ascended the skies.

He gazed upon the still blue ocean
reflecting the firmament
watching the Flower of Flowers
become but a tiny speck of light
which suddenly shone
as the most brilliant star in all the heavens.

The Golden Eagle flew so effortlessly
ascending the skies
gliding in ever increasing circles
to the whim of the wind's caress.

Johnnie smiled at the Child King
feeling he must explode with joy
upon this most wondrous of all journeys
when he gazed below him incredulous
for from out of the depths
of the great ocean
arose the Earth in all her splendour.

The Sun and Moon shone
adorning the darkness with light
offering their most gracious welcome
while the waters of the great ocean
fell as a sparkling garland of pearls.

34

Johnnie was witness of a new day dawning.

Cascading waterfalls
descending in thunderous mists
exploding
the beginnings of mighty rivers.
The birth of clouds and rains.
Rivulets and streams
winding through newly formed
valleys and plains.
Flowing waters seeking
through the earth the seas.
The ocean.
The rainbow-colours of creation
manifesting their myriad of forms.
Waters
teeming with all manner of life.
Fishes great and small.
Forests of trees
grasses
heather and wild.
Flowers in the bloom of eternal hue.
Lands and skies
graced with all mammals
animals and birds of the imagination.

Magical realms and kingdoms
filled and flowing
with the splendour and glory of all peoples.

Such was the wonder
that befell Johnnie's eyes.

Such was the vision
in the Child King's eyes.

The Golden Eagle
encircled the Earth once more
gliding gracefully
to alight upon a white sandy shore.

Johnnie placed his feet upon white sands
marvelling
of the wonder of the sights he had seen.

The great bird bowed graciously
eyes smiling as he flew into the distance
just as he had come
only now alight
like a bright guiding star in the heavens.

The Silent Ocean

"Johnnie."

Once more he discerned of the sound
of the Mother's voice calling.

Tinkle ...

　　　Tinkle ...

　　　　　Tinkle ...

The glory of the heavens were mirrored
in their most perfect reflection
upon the deepest blue waters of the Silent Ocean
lapping gently before him.

For a moment
he remained upon the bright white sands
gazing in awe upon the great ocean and skies
marvelling of their grandeur
and perhaps it was this awe
this grandeur
that reawakened the fear in his heart.

The vast majesty
that made him aware of his helplessness
of his being alone
and he knew now that somehow the fear
that was filling his heart must be overcome.

He gazed once more
upon the glistening waters of the great ocean
knowing he must cross over it
though he knew not how.

"Johnnie."

Suddenly from nowhere
he heard the sound of the Child King's voice.

"You may cross the ocean as you wish.
This is simply a dream.
The ocean does not exist.

Have faith in your self!"

Johnnie was puzzled by these words
totally unaware that he was dreaming.
To him the ocean seemed very real.
However
although he may be unsure of himself
he had faith in the Child King
and so boldly he marched towards the ocean
when ...

SPLASH

Coughing and spluttering and a little shaken and wet
he made his way back to the shore.

He sat for a while until he was dry.

A little confused.

Perhaps he should close his eyes
and pretend the ocean did not exist.
So closing his eyes
and slightly less boldly than before
he marched towards the ocean
when ...

SPLASH

Perhaps he should try running.

SPLASH

Ah! What if he jumped?

SPLASH

With one eye open?

SPLASH

With one eye closed?

SPLASH

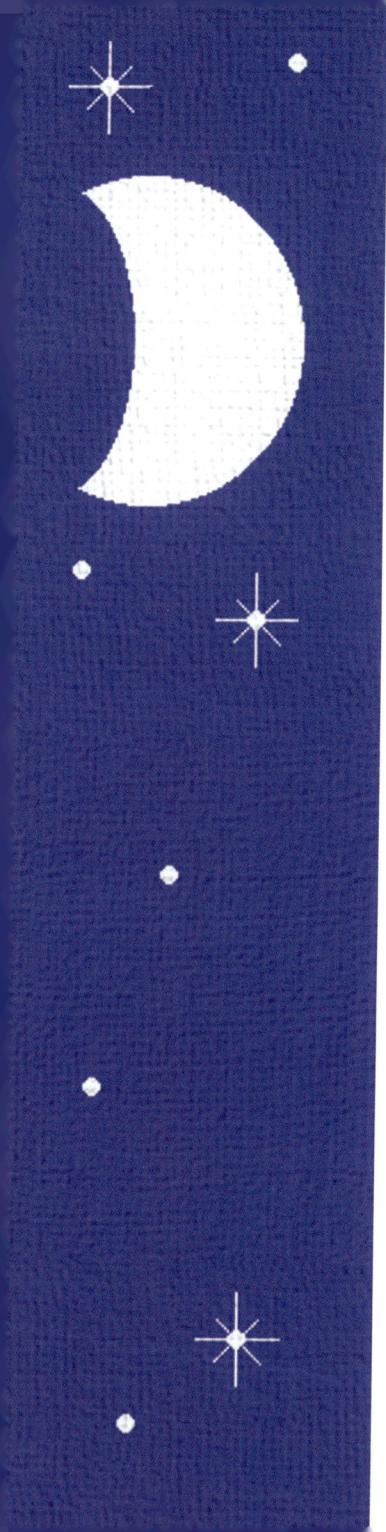

"Aaaaaaaaaaaah!"

SPLASH

He was very confused now
for if this was truly a dream
and the ocean did not exist
why was he soaking wet?

It all seemed too real.

Johnnie began to despair
for try as he may
he could not make unreal
what he perceived to be very real.

Tinkle ...

Tinkle ...

Tinkle ...

"Johnnie."

He looked out across the ocean
and there upon the waves appeared the Child King
smiling and calling his name
untroubled by the waters which were simply his support.

In that moment Johnnie forgot the obstacle of the ocean
and his heart so full of joy of this wondrous sight
seemed to guide him across the waters
to where the Child King stood.
But as he moved forward to greet him
he was not there.
It was as if he had passed through him.
He looked all around
but there was no sign of the Child King
and to his great surprise the ocean lay behind him.
He had crossed the waters though he knew not how.

He began to smile as he envisioned the Child King
and wondered at the sweet play of this Divine Child.

The Battle

"Johnnie."

Once more he discerned of the sound
of the Mother's voice calling.
It seemed so gentle.
So near and so far away.
Yet he was aware of Her Presence
as though She was both within
and all around him protecting and guiding.
This made him feel very secure
for now he was all alone
or at least so he thought.

As he stood upon the bright white sands
he mused on the vision before him.
Upon either side of the horizon
two regal mountains began their noble ascent
sweeping graciously aside to offer sight
of the most majestic Snowy Mountain
ascending the distance before them.

rustle rustle rustle

Johnnie heard a sound
a faint echo filling the space all around him.

46

He stopped and slowly studied each direction.
Listening.
All was so very still.

He returned his gaze to the grace of the Snowy Mountain
knowing he must journey to that place.

(FLASH)

There was a flash of light somewhere in the distance.

(FLASH)

Followed by another

(FLASH)

and another like the twinkling of a star
although Johnnie was aware this was no star twinkling.

murmur murmur murmur

More sound, almost inaudible but moving closer

murmur murmur murmur

and closer still.

47

The

rustle rustle rustle

was now accompanied with a

THUNDER-RUMBLE

The ground appeared to shudder beneath him and the

RUSTLE RUSTLE RUSTLE
MURMUR MURMUR MURMUR

was becoming louder and louder.
A mist of dust was rising in the valley before him.

(FLASH)

Flashes of light like bolts of lighting pierced the dust-mist
as the thunder rumbled and a sound like stomping feet

THUD THUD THUD
THUD THUD THUD
THUD THUD THUD

trampled the earth like some crazed monster
hell-bent on destruction.

CLINK-CLANK CLINK-CLANK

The clinking of metal and the clanking of steel
sounded from the dust-mist rising ever higher and higher
and the

THUNDER-RUMBLE
RUSTLE RUSTLE RUSTLE
(FLASH)
MURMUR MURMUR MURMUR

grew ever louder
moving ever closer.
Filling the air with a tremendous noise
and dust and light.
If Johnnie had not felt afraid before he did now
for from within the dust-mist emerged
the most horrible snarling war-clad army
moving menacingly towards him.
He did not know what to do.
He could not run.
There was nowhere to run to.
Behind him lay the great ocean
and before him stood the Snarling Army
surrounding him upon all sides
and there were so many of them.
He could not move.

49

Tinkle ...

  Tinkle ...

    Tinkle ...

"Johnnie."

Above the clamour of the approaching army
he heard the sound of the tinkling bell
and a voice calling his name.

He turned once more
to find the Child King by his side
smiling.

In his eyes there was no fear
and so calmly he spoke these words.

"Johnnie

there is no cause to be afraid
Mother would not allow you to be harmed.
Be strong.

Let us stand and prepare to do Battle."

He felt the fear in him subside
as he witnessed the Child King
resplendent
in an armour of red-gold regalia.
In whose hands he beheld
a great bow
a shining spear
and a glittering sword
and whose shoulders bore a bejewelled quiver
filled to flowing with golden arrows
and a light -
a light which appeared to emanate
the Child King's presence
glowing all around him.
Johnnie looked
and to his amazement was aware
that he too was clad in just such an armour
when ...

THUNDER-RUMBLE
(FLASH)
RUSTLE RUSTLE RUSTLE
CLINK-CLANK CLINK-CLANK
MURMUR MURMUR MURMUR

the most horrible Snarling Army began their march.

THUD!
THUD THUD THUD

AAAEEEAAARRREEEAAAGGG!

Shouting and screaming as the dust-mist
rose all around them concealing their presence.

THUD!
THUD THUD THUD

The noise grew louder and louder.

THUNDER-RUMBLE
(FLASH)
RUSTLE RUSTLE RUSTLE
CLINK-CLANK CLINK-CLANK
MURMUR MURMUR MURMUR

The dust-mist moved closer and closer.

THUD!
THUD THUD THUD
THUD!
THUD THUD THUD
THUD!
THUD THUD THUD
THUD!

With this final

THUD!

the earth shuddered and was still.
The dust-mist rose to reveal the most horrible snarling foe
filling the stillness with an icy terror
and although Johnnie felt secure in the Child King's presence
his heart began beating faster and faster.
So much so that he felt he must explode
when ...

THUD!
THUD THUD THUD
THUD!
THUD THUD THUD
THUD!
THUD THUD THUD

The Snarling Army began stamping their feet.
The dust-mist gathered.

THUD!
THUD THUD THUD

The earth was trembling.
The ocean and the skies were trembling.
Johnnie was trembling.

53

The Child King was smiling
and reassured him

"Johnnie
 do not be afraid.

 All is being taken care of."

In that moment a light surrounded them
and nestled in this presence he felt secure.
He looked to the Child King
and they both began to smile.

Suddenly ...

CHHHAAARRRGGGE!

came a deafening roar.

THUD!
THUD THUD THUD

From out of the dust-mist charged
the Snarling Army.

Tinkle ...

Tinkle ...

Tinkle ...

He turned to the Child King in whose eyes
the light shone
brighter than the brightest star.
So much so
he imagined himself to be part of this light.

Johnnie closed his eyes and took a deep breath
and when he opened them
the Child King smiled at him and said

"Ready?"

He closed his eyes once more
and taking another deep breath smiled inside
bowing to affirm
Yes
Yes he was . . .

"Ready!"

Johnnie opened his eyes to see by his side
the most amazing Monkey Warrior
attired in red-gold regalia.
Beholding a great bow
a shining spear
and a glittering sword
and whose shoulders bore a bejewelled quiver
filled to flowing with golden arrows.

A mirror reflection of the Child King and himself
and although he had never seen
the Monkey Warrior before
he imagined he must have known him forever.
For within his eyes a light shone
just like the light
that shone in the Child King's eyes.

Just like the light that had begun his journey.

The light that he felt to be all around.
A part of him and he a part of it.

How the three stood
resplendent
in the face of their oncoming foe.

Lightning flashing
from the tips of their swords
their spears
and their golden arrows
and it was as if
that for a moment upon seeing them
the Snarling Army's step faltered

but it was only for a moment.

CHHHAAARRRGGGE!

On they came closer and closer.

THUD!
THUD THUD THUD
THUD!
THUD THUD THUD
THUD!
THUD THUD THUD

Tinkle ...

        Tinkle ...

                Tinkle ...

All was silent
and from within the Silence Johnnie imagined
he had been given complete protection.
For upon either side of him stood most glorious
the Child King and the Monkey Warrior.
Before him
beyond the face of the oncoming foe
ascended the most majestic Snowy Mountain
like a Father.
A silent witness over all.

Behind him lay the great ocean.

But much more than this
a presence
such as a Mother watching over Her children.
Protecting and guiding
with Her Love filling them completely
and who would never allow any harm to befall them.
Within the Silence of that moment
he began to understand the Child King's words.

CHHHAAARRRGGGE!

His reverie was broken.

SSSTHTHWWIIISSSHHH

The air was filled with the sound
of a wave of the Snarling Army's arrows dazzling the skies.
The Child King and Monkey Warrior looked to Johnnie.
The three bowed, drew back their great bows and

SSSTHTHWWIIISSSHHH

a brilliant shower of golden arrows filled the skies
easily combatting the dazzling array
of enemy arrows zooming towards them.
Cutting through their offence
to land upon the farthest legions
who upon being struck caused to spark a light
vanishing from sight within puffs of smoke.
Thus, with each dazzling foray of enemy arrows

SSSTHTHWWIIISSSHHH

a shower of golden arrows
with ease would banish them from the skies
when ...

SSSZZZZSSSZZZZSSS

The skies were ablaze with a flaming mass of spears.
In an instance the Child King, Monkey Warrior and Johnnie
returned their fire with a luminous veil of golden spears
easily staying the Snarling Army's attack.
Only this time falling upon the inner legions of their foe
who were vanquished within the luminous glare
of brilliant bolts of lightning, and so it was that with each

SSSTHTHWWIIISSSHHH

of the Snarling Army's arrows
the Child King, Monkey Warrior and Johnnie would reply

SSSTHTHWWIIISSSHHH

with a brilliant shower of golden arrows
rendering their weapons and their legions obsolete
within sparks of light and puffs of smoke, and with each

SSSZZZZSSSZZZZSSS

of the blazing mass of the Snarling Army's flaming spears
the three with a luminous veil of golden spears

SSSZZZZSSSZZZZSSS

would banish the attack
piercing their ranks and destroying their legions
within the luminous glare of bolts of lightning.

Yet something strange

something very strange was happening.

For although the many legions
of the ranks of the Snarling Army
were being vanquished
and their numbers were diminishing
those soldiers that remained
were growing in size
as if absorbing all those that had gone before.
Until before them
stood snarling
three enormous figures whose monstrous presence
loomed over them
causing a twilight to descend the earth.

CHHHAAARRRGGGE!

The three monstrous figures drew their swords
and lunged
at the Child King, Monkey Warrior and Johnnie
who in an instance
as one
unsheathed their glittering swords and

CLANK-CHINK
(FLASH)
CHINK-CLANK
(FLASH)
CHINK-CLANK-CLANK-CHINK
(FLASH)

how the sparks flew
exploding in pockets of light and dark
and how the three fought
swords clashing
flashing the illumined twilight.

CHINK-CLANK
(FLASH)
CLANK-CHINK
(FLASH)
CLANK-CHINK-CHINK-CLANK
(FLASH)

Johnnie imagined
that his sword must be guided by an unseen hand
for with such swiftness of ease and grace
did he combat his foe
when ...

AAARRRGGGHHH!

a sound like thunder shook the earth, seas and skies
as the Child King, Monkey Warrior and Johnnie
in a single movement
pierced the hearts of their menacing foes.

LIGHT

then

DARKNESS

For before them stood the single most monstrous being
causing the earth to darkness.
The most fearsome combination of all that had gone before
and Johnnie imagined that all of the fear
he had known within his heart now appeared before him
laughing.

AAA-HAAA-HAAA-HAAA

Eyes and teeth snarling as he threw back his head

AAA-HAAA-HAAA-HAAA

and raising his foot as if to crush the three beneath him.

AAA-HAAA-HAAA-HAAA

Tinkle ...

        Tinkle ...

                Tinkle ...

"Now Johnnie!"

A voice calmly spoke.

Without a thought
just as the monstrous foot
was about to crash down upon him
Johnnie shot a single golden arrow
guided by his desire.
In that moment
the Child King hurled a golden spear
and Monkey Warrior threw a glittering sword.

Suddenly from within their hearts as one
a tiny ball of flame soared
uniting the tips of the three weapons
and the Snarling Monster upon seeing this
stumbled back flailing his arms.

AAARRRGGGHHH!

The earth, seas and skies shuddered
filled with the sound of roaring thunder
for try as he might
he could not deter the flame-illumined weapons
which flew like a comet straight into his heart.

AAARRRGGGHHH!

The earth, seas and skies shook one last time
as the flame
arrow
spear and sword
were emblazoned upon the Snarling Monster's breast
drawing his body into the light
and the monstrous enemy was absorbed
into the flame
until not a piece of him remained.

From within the light came a single implosion.

BAABOOOOM

Like a final heartbeat
followed by a silent explosion of brilliant light.

The most beautiful of all light.

Tinkle ...

Tinkle ...

Tinkle ...

The tiny bell sounded
and the universe was alive with a magical melody.
The earth, the ocean and the skies
a shimmering majesty of light.

Johnnie looked at the Child King and Monkey Warrior
and then at himself
for they were no longer dressed for war
but simply attired as three small children.
They smiled and bowed together
laughing and singing as they began the Dance of Song
and how they danced and danced in circles
spiralling the firmament in a celestial play.

Sharing in this moment of eternity
until finally alighting upon bright white sands.

Monkey Warrior smiled
and bowed to Johnnie and the Child King
who smiled and bowed to Monkey Warrior
but when they looked up he was gone.

There was a brilliant flash of light
and the heavens were adorned with the brightest star.

The Golden Flute

Johnnie turned to the Child King
in whose hands he beheld a gift of gold.
The Child King smiled and bowed
presenting him with a Golden Flute
light as the air
carved to simple perfection
with seven holes sparkling like seven stars.

He smiled and bowed
graciously accepting the gift
and although he knew not
how to play such an instrument
he mused on her beauty
but when Johnnie looked up
the Child King was gone.

The whole world seemed brighter now
lit with a light emanating joy
and it seemed
that from the source of this joy
the Child King's voice spoke a single word

"Listen."

He sat down upon bright white sands
to peruse the Golden Flute
adorned with the lights of the seven stars
and he wondered of their sound.

All was so silent.
The world shone all around him

and he listened . . .

Suddenly from nowhere
a gentle breeze blew
and the sound grew all around him

and he listened . . .

Johnnie gazed upon the first hole
and wondered
is this where I must place my lips
to blow such as the gentle breeze?
For the breeze borne of the Silence
must be the root of the sound.
The wings upon which she flies.

He placed the Golden Flute to his lips
and with all his fingers raised
he began to softly blow.
The sound of the gentle breeze
breathed as his breath
so silent
so low
rising higher and higher
and as he listened to the flow
the breath and the breeze were one.

Johnnie smiled.

A shiver of joy flowed through him
as he
absorbed within the depths
of this most sacred sound
perceived of the starlit heavens
the shimmering ocean
and the burnished earth most glorious.

All was silent

and he listened . . .

Johnnie mused as a gentle breeze blew
weaving
a mystery dance across the ocean.

Ripples great and small graced her depths.
Waves rose and fell
splashing upon bright white sands.
Splintered sea spray
sprinkled all around him
resplendent
against the gaze of the Sun and Moon.

He perused the second hole
of the Golden Flute
lit
with the light of the ocean
and placing his finger
upon the shimmering star
he gently blew
the nuances of movement and sound
flowing through him.

From tiny drop to mighty ocean.
Mists to clouds.
Raindrops to rainfall
falling
like sacred showers upon the earth.
Babbling brooks
rivulets and streams.
Flowing rivers
upon their sojourn of the seas.

He was all of these
borne
of the depths of the ocean's mystery
singing through him her song of eternity
and with his breath upon the Golden Flute
he breathed
her Silence and her sound

the ocean manifesting

and he listened . . .

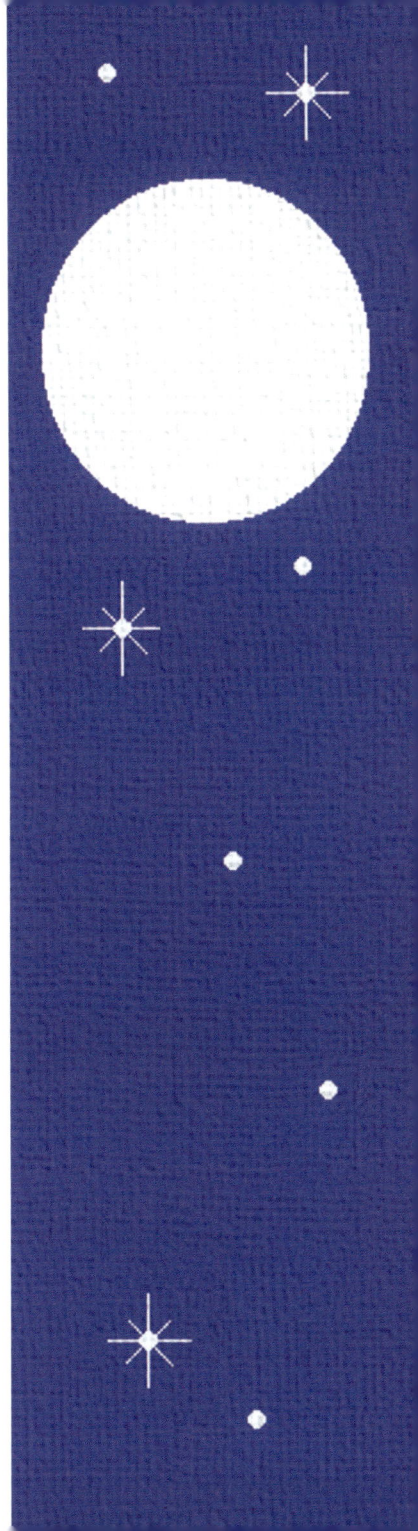

Arising he turned his gaze
from the ocean
marvelling
of the Snowy Mountain
gracing the distance before him
while the feeling
that he must journey there
grew in his heart.

He turned once more
and bowing his head bade farewell
to the great ocean
knowing she existed within him.

He stepped away
from the bright white sands
to a dust-red road
Golden Flute in hand

journeying his sojourn of sound

and he listened . . .

Walking upon the dust-red road
he perceived of a landscape
adorned
with myriad grasses and wild.

Flowers radiant in bloom
swayed
to a silent melody
showering fields and meadow-glades
hills and dales.

He glided the way before him
while the red dust rose
with every footstep he may take.

All of nature was dancing.

The breeze rustling petals
and ruffling leaves
of the flowers and trees
in a meandering rainbow-wave
of colour and sound.

Johnnie gazed upon the third hole
and nature's star shone in his eyes
as he raised the Golden Flute to his lips
and blew softly the world before him.

The whisper of his breath
as the breeze
flowed across the grasses and wild
through the flowers and trees.

In every stirring
in all of these
he was filled to flowing
with every nuance
of every movement of every sound.

The dreamscape lived within him
in her ever changing form
until with the many sounds
and the many forms he became one

and he listened . . .

He looked to the horizon
and to the path
ascending the Snowy Mountain

his feet
gliding the dust-red road.

Realms and kingdoms appeared before him
upon his journey of the people

though they may not see him

and as he walked unnoticed in their midst
he listened to their life.

From the first breath
crying tears of wonder
of the world to which they have come.

To the last breath
held in wonder
of the world to which they were departing.

He journeyed the way of the people
and the times of their lives.
Learning
of each and every soul
from the very young to the very old
through
laughter and tears
glory and pain
joy and sorrow.

His life was theirs as theirs was his.

The dream.

The vision.

He listened to the rhythm
of their heartbeat
beating
within his heart beating
within the heart of hearts.

A lone witness of the light
that shone
within each and every one.

Sitting down in their midst
he mused upon the fourth hole
of the Golden Flute
resplendent
as a starlit wish
and he imagined the breath of life
to be born here
as he raised her to his lips.

He blew softly a melody of song
and the melody flowed as a wave
rippling the depths of the Silence
in search of distant shores.
A never-ending song of love
sent as a guide for the journey.

The unique sojourn of the soul.

Johnnie walked from their midst
with the song of life
singing in his heart
and though they may not see him
he bowed bidding farewell
knowing the light of their life
shone within him.

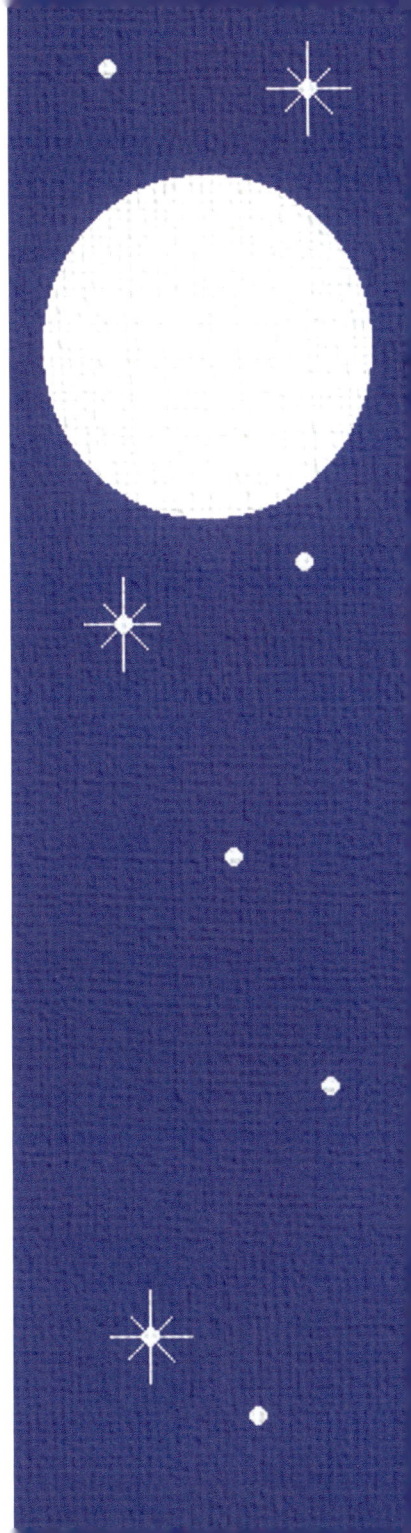

He placed his feet upon the path
gliding
an illumined landscape

splintered red dust rose behind him

and he listened . . .

He journeyed the way that led from the people.

The Snowy Mountain
bright white
shone in the distance before him.

A gentle breeze blew
revealing a sound so beautiful
he halted his steps
and the melody wrapped all around him
raising and carrying him
in a tender embrace.

Floating above the dust-red road
he was witness to a world
radiating
the harmonies
of an ancient song of songs
when suddenly
there appeared before him
a mighty tree lit with the lights
of the colours of the rainbow.

Each light a leaf
each rustling leaf a voice

a unique melody

and with each breath of the breeze
a shimmering rainbow-wave
of colour and sound
rippled
the branches and leaves of the tree.

Johnnie gazed into the tree
to where the purest light shone
which as he moved nearer
appeared as a soul-white Dove.

Still the music carried him
closer and closer
when from within the heart
of the soul-white Dove
he discerned
of the most silent explosion.

Light

and colour-scattered rainbow-leaves
adorned the world before him

each leaf a songbird singing
a unique melody.

Their silent wings upon the breeze
sprinkled the heavens
each one borne
upon the wings of the other
in an eternal flow of harmony.

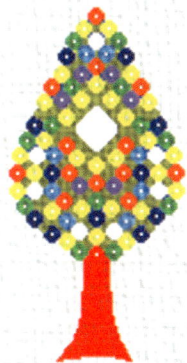

The sound of the music grew
and grew
reaching a crescendo
while the many birds
in their many colours flew
encircling the heavens one last time
to alight upon the tree.

Once more
as shimmering rainbow-leaves
of light.

Illumined within the heart of the tree
the soul-white Dove shone
while the song of songs
flowed through him
in her nuances of colour and sound.

Johnnie gazed upon the fifth hole
aflame
with soul-light
and raising the Golden Flute to his lips
with his breath he breathed
the eternal flow of harmony.

How he flew
gracing the firmament's gaze
upon the wings of light
gliding
the colours of the rainbow.

He lowered the Golden Flute
to perceive of the splendour
of the soul-white Dove
the shimmering colours
of the rainbow tree of life
and his becoming
the silent flight of the song of songs.

He bowed bidding farewell
and placing his foot upon the dust-red road
he moved beyond the tree
while all around him
the world was flowing with the melody
of a new song of songs.

The Tree of Life bloomed within him

and he listened . . .

The Snowy Mountain
rose
blossoming the world before him.

Each moment of each movement
simply adding to the grandeur
of the ascending majesty
of ancient rock and stone
rising and falling
with every footstep he may take
gliding
the dust-red road to his goal.

Through forests and meadow-glades
valleys and dales.
Wandering the meandering river.
Reflecting upon mirror lakes
while ever in sight
of the glistening waters of the seas.
Over sands and dune deserts
to an oasis and an ancient well
where in Silence
he offered his most secret wish.

Suddenly he stood at the foot
of the Snowy Mountain
gazing in awe of the silent majesty
of ancient rock and stone
white snows and white snow-clouds
and he wondered
how may he ascend such a way?

Snow-white heights emblazoned
with moon-sun-light reached out to him.

"This way!"
"This way!"

Two voices were calling to him
from either side of the mountain.

"This way Johnnie. This way!"
"This way Johnnie. This way!"

Two roads diverged from the place
where he stood
encircling the mountain upon either side.
Rising and falling as they wove their way
through ancient rock to fade
into the mists
of snow-clouds and silent stone.

Would one of them lead him to the snowy peak?
He did not know.

"This way Johnnie. This way!
Follow.
Climb upon the wings of What Was
and you will surely have reached your goal."

"This way Johnnie. This way!
Follow.
Climb upon the wings of What Will Be
and you will surely reach your goal."

The voices were becoming louder and louder.

"This way!"
"This way!"

He imagined the voices to be inside
like two parts of himself
pulling in opposite directions.
But which way should he follow?
In his heart he wished to journey forward
but the rise of the ancient rock
seemed to deny his desire.

He perused the emblazoned heights.

"This way Johnnie. This way!

Through all that was
seek the hidden treasures
of the distant past
that you may master the path
that will lead you to your goal.

Do not deny what was your destiny."

"This way Johnnie. This way!

Through all that will be
seek the glittering prizes found
through the unfolding of the future
and you will be master of the path
that will lead you to your goal.

Do not deny what was to be your destiny."

Two great forces were tugging at his being
and he felt very confused
for of the two directions
which one should he follow?

From the way of What Was
arose a light tinged sleepy-dreamy
luring a part of him to sleep
dreaming
of the hidden treasures of the past.

While from the way of What Will Be
arose a light tinged restless-waking
causing him to awake in a flight of fancy
racing headlong
after the glittering prizes of the future.

"This way!"
"This way!"

The voices became
louder
then softer
more persuasive and more subtle.

"This way Johnnie. This way!"
"This way Johnnie. This way!"

Until he imagined he must be torn in two.

Tinkle ...

       Tinkle ...

             Tinkle ...

The tiny bell sounded
and for a moment all was calm and still.

The Child King's voice spoke to him
saying

"Johnnie.

Listen
within the Silence of your heart speaking
and you may choose your true path."

He listened to his heart
and all he knew was that his deepest wish
was to journey forward

to ascend the illumined heights.

He did not wish to know of What Was
or What Will Be but to know What Is.

In that moment the voices ceased.

Johnnie stepped forward
as if two parts of himself had fallen away
and in the lightness of his being
he tripped lithely the ancient rock and stone.

Ascending in a moment the snowy peak.

Now amidst the still of white snowflakes
dancing
he gazed below upon the two roads
encircling the mountain to meet
at the place where he once stood.

He sat down
safe in his silent white space
adorned with the light of the Sun and Moon

and he listened . . .

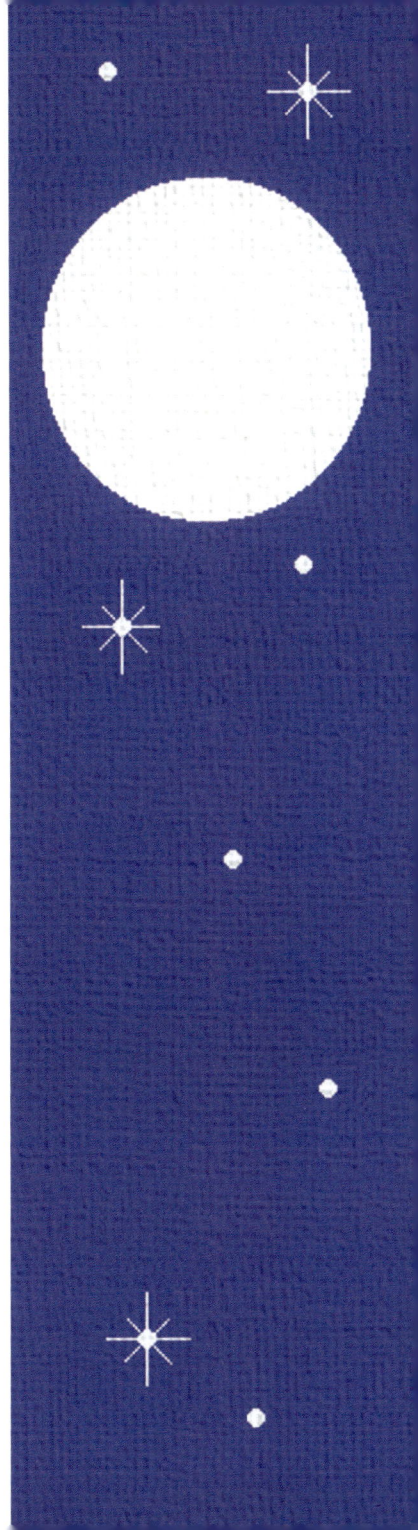

All was so serene
so calm
so clear.
His being drenched in the rays
of the Sun and Moon
and for a moment
Johnnie wondered of his journey to this place
and where he must go from here.

Was he where he should be?

A hint of doubt arose clouding his vision.
He seemed so very alone
here upon the snow white height
and what if he should fall?

All was not so clear now
for many clouds were forming
filling the silent space before him
and the thoughts began to play with him.

Should he have taken one of the other paths?

Suddenly he was filled with doubt.

*"What if I had taken the path of
What Waaaaaaaaaaaaah!"*

Suddenly he was falling
tumbling
down the side of the mountain
only to be caught by the Child King
and returned to the snowy peak.

Again a doubt arose.

*"What if I had taken the Path of
What Will Beeeeeeeeeeeeh!"*

Now he was falling
tumbling
down the other side of the mountain.
Only this time he was caught by Monkey Warrior
and swiftly returned to the snowy peak.
So it was
that many times clouded in moments of doubt
he would fall and each time be caught
and safely returned to the snowy peak
by either the Child King or Monkey Warrior.

Tinkle ...

Tinkle ...

Tinkle ...

Once more the tiny bell sounded
and the voice of the Child King spoke
saying

"Johnnie
there is no need for any thoughts
for such are clouds of doubt.

You are where you chose to be.

Listen within your Silence
and you may complete your journey."

He gazed upon the light of the Sun and Moon
shining before him
and if he listened so very carefully
he could discern of the sound
of the ethereal breeze
guiding them upon their path in the heavens.

He perused the sixth hole
of the Golden Flute
lit with moon-sun-light
and with his breath he breathed
the ethereal breeze
and the light of silent reflection.

The Sun and Moon graced the firmament
with their ancient mystery dance
revealing their glory and majesty
through the melody of song.

He was one with the reflected light
of their perfection
that shone so brightly within him
and the sound of the ethereal breeze
that wove an ancient melody through him
flowing
as his breath upon the Golden Flute.

Johnnie stood upon the highest height
as the Sun and Moon
shone within and all around him

and he listened . . .

Within the Silence of snowflakes
dancing
he looked beyond the Sun and Moon
to a tiny spark of flame
and from within the light-flame
bloomed a garden
amidst whose falling leaves
children were playing
dancing and singing.

The garden entrance
was adorned with a garland of light
before which stood the Child King
whose smile lit the heavens
as with these words he spoke

*"Johnnie
you may come home now."*

He smiled.
A tear of joy fell from his eyes
and from where the teardrop
touched upon white snows
there appeared a rainbow.
A sacred bridge bowing the heavens
from the place where he stood
to the gateway of the Silent Garden.

He gazed upon the seventh hole
of the Golden Flute
emblazoned
with the colours of the rainbow
and to the soul-white Dove
who was at rest upon the instrument
and whose light shone brightly in his eyes.

Upon slowly closing and opening his eyes
he perceived of the light of her presence
both within and without his being
as though he was nothing but the light
and within that moment
the soul-white Dove took flight
and flew upon the colours of the rainbow
and beyond
to merge with the source of the Silent Garden.

He knew now her source.
He knew now her wingéd flight.

Johnnie pressed the Golden Flute to his lips
as he danced lightly the way before him
and with his breath he breathed
the sounds of the colours of the rainbow.

The breath of the breeze.
The great ocean.
The waters flowing.
The winds, storms and seas.
The dream meadow-glade, grasses and wild.
The flowers, petals and leaves of the trees.
The silent heartbeat.
The breath of life.
The people, their laughter and tears.
The rainbow tree of life.
The colour-birds of rainbow-leaves.
The soul-white Dove.
The mountain, snow and snowflakes dancing.
The ethereal breeze.
The Sun and Moon and stars.
The sacred rainbow.
The wingéd flight.
The Silence.

All nuances of colour and sound
upon the breath of the breeze
flowed through him
while his fingers danced upon the stars.
He had become the flute of gold
and the spontaneous flow of the song of eternity.

He stood below the garland of light
at the gateway to the Silent Garden
and as he smiled and bowed to the Child King
he marvelled to see him becoming
the Child of Ages.
The eternal youth in whose eyes
the light of the Child King shone.

The Child of Ages smiled and embraced Johnnie

"You are home now"

he seemed to say though no words were spoken.

The gateway opened and he was in awe
of the vision before him.

The Silence of the song of eternity
wove her melody
through gracelight-illumined leaves
dancing upon the breeze like shooting stars
all around him
and within their midst children were playing
dancing and singing.

He could not move
for how may he enter this realm of beauty?

The Silent Garden

Tender light-showers fell all around him
drenching his senses.
Still he could not move.
He was immersed in the beauty.
When suddenly
from the midst of the children playing
a young girl ran towards him
and with her bright eyes shining
she appeared as a mirror.
His soul reflection.
She moved towards him smiling
and taking his hand
she led him into the Silent Garden
and into the midst of children playing
who in their joy upon seeing him
embraced him as one.

Johnnie perceived of a flame
that shone within his heart
and when he looked upon the girl
so the flame shone in her heart as his.
Shining
within the heart of each and every child
and in their eyes a light -
the light that had begun his journey.
They were all
brothers and sisters of the Silence.

Johnnie was home.

Tinkle ...

       Tinkle ...

              Tinkle ...

The tiny bell sounded.
The children gathered and with one voice
they breathed the most silent sound
resounding Johnnie's being.
A magical melody played
heralding the Dance of Song
while the children wove the eternal circle.

The girl smiled and took his hand
leading him within the circle
where with all the children
they began dancing and singing
in the midst of golden-leaf-light-showers
falling all around them.

Once more he was witness of the flame
that shone within the heart of all
and in this moment
he perceived of the grace and beauty
of the Child King and the Child of Ages
pervading the Silence
with their presence eternal.

Still the melody flowed
when he realised
he was leading the circle of dance.

The children illumined in light
wove gracefully
within and without one another
spiralling the garden.

Johnnie was entering the Silence
of the centre of the circle
and as he did so
he began to rise
as though drawn to the source.

All around him
children were happily dancing
holding hands and weaving circles
like flame-lit haloes
encircling the circle of eternity.

The light grew brighter
as he rose higher
and higher
entering the depths
of the source of the Silence.

Johnnie rose ascending the circle
while the children
swirling like light-flames
shone brightly all around him.

He was being filled with light
and a sound so silent.

Gazing upon his soul reflection
he knew that they were one
and in that moment
within the light of her eyes shining as his
he let go of her hand
and she appeared as the flame
that in his eyes shone.

He rose ascending the source.

Higher and higher as illumined light.

Deeper and deeper
as the numinous depths of Silence.

Tinkle ...

        Tinkle ...

                Tinkle ...

"Wake up."

The Mother's voice was softly calling.

"Wake up Johnnie."

Johnnie opened and closed his eyes
as moon-sun-light streamed in
through open windows
and the light shone within him as without.

He began to rub his eyes
as he gazed upon a face

so peaceful
so Divine

shining brighter than the brightest star
as though She was the source of the light itself

and as he perceived of Her beauty
shining within him
he knew his self to be born of this light.
To be born of Her Love.

Now he understood the words
the Child King had spoken.

She had been with him
upon each and every step of his journey.

His guide and his protection.

She the Mother of all Her children
and he knew

She was his Mother too!

He embraced his Mother in joy
and illumined in the light of Her Love
he ran to the door.

This he opened slowly
as moon-sun-light streamed in
uniting with the inner light of his life.

This was his true home.

He moved to the gate and gazed beyond
upon the way that lay before him.

Johnnie turned to his Mother and smiled
and opened the gate to walk through
for placing his foot upon the path he knew
this moment was his Gift to life.

His moment of beauty.

His moment of perfection.

The Beginning

Lightning Source UK Ltd.
Milton Keynes UK
UKIC02n2131011214
242490UK00011B/103